I REALLY want the cake!

Simon Philip

Lucia Gaggiotti

templar
books

There's a smell I can't ignore.
It's wafting through the kitchen door.
It's time for me to find out more.

NEW ♥ ECO style

BRUNO MUNARI

I think . . .

. . . it might be cake.

It's on the table sitting there.
I cannot help but stop and stare.
And now I'm really quite aware . . .

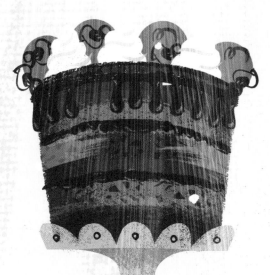

. . . I think I want
the cake.

The decoration's just so neat.
That icing looks like such a treat.
It smells so chocolatey and sweet!

I want it now, and though I'm small,
I'm sure that I could scoff it all.
But Mum has written in a scrawl . . .

I'd be a fool to disobey.
To eat the cake is **not** okay.
And maybe if I go away . . .

. . . I might forget the cake.

I'm really trying to be strong.
To eat it would be very wrong.
I've wanted it for so, so long!

I must . . .

. . . forget the cake.

That thought has made me rather glum,
and all I want is one small crumb.

I might ignore the note from Mum.

It's still there waiting, nicely placed
for me to have a little taste.

To leave it would be **such** a waste.
I'll only lick the cake.

Oh my, oh my! What a delight!

Somehow the lick became a bite.

I can't control my appetite.

Just one more slice of cake.

I know I've not been very wise.
And what I've done I can't disguise.
I might have to apologise . . .

. . . because I ate the cake.

Oh, silly me! What have I done?
I'll have to make another one.
I guess it could be kind of fun.

I've never **baked** a cake.

I need some eggs! I'll start with six.
It's sure to be a tasty mix.
There's nothing that I cannot fix!
It's **easy** making cake!

I'll whisk and beat and stir and shake
until my arms begin to ache . . .
Oh no! That wasn't meant to break!

It's **hard** to make a cake!

My gosh, the **mess!** It's everywhere.
It's up the walls and in my hair.
When Mum sees this she'll faint, I swear.
It's chaos making cake!

Hi Mum, I've come here to confess.
I'm sorry if I've caused you stress.
And yes, I've made a lot of mess . . .

. . . but **hey**, I've made
you cake!

For Morgan, Iris, Derek and Angela,
for all your love, encouragement and cakes!
SP

All my love to my nephew, Alessandro,
who is sweet like chocolate!
LG

A TEMPLAR BOOK

First published in the UK in 2017 by Templar Publishing,
an imprint of Kings Road Publishing, part of the Bonnier Publishing Group,
The Plaza, 535 King's Road, London, SW10 0SZ
www.bonnierpublishing.com

Text copyright © 2017 by Simon Philip
Illustration copyright © 2017 by Lucia Gaggiotti
Design copyright © 2017 by The Templar Company Limited

3 5 7 9 10 8 6 4

ISBN 978-1-78370-801-7

This book was typeset in Brandon Grotesque
The illustrations were created with collage and digital medium

Designed by Genevieve Webster
Edited by Katie Haworth

Printed in China

I Really Want the Chocolate Cake

Do you **really** want a cake? Here is a recipe to try at home.
Remember to ask a grown-up to help you! This cake is **excellent** for
people but is **not to be given to dogs.**

For the cake

- 230g/8oz plain flour
- 350g/12oz white sugar
- 80g/3oz cocoa powder
- 1½ tsp baking powder
- 1½ tsp bicarbonate of soda
- 2 eggs
- 250ml/8fl milk
- 125ml/4fl vegetable oil
- 50g/2oz chocolate, melted

For the icing

- 150g/5oz butter
- 2 tbsp cocoa powder
- 300g/10oz icing sugar

1. Preheat the oven to 180°C/350°F.

2. Grease two 20cm/8in cake tins and line the bottom with baking paper.

3. Sift dry ingredients into a large mixing bowl.

4. Add eggs, vegetable oil and milk and mix until you have a smooth batter.

5. Mix in melted chocolate last.

6. Pour batter in the two tins and then bake for 30 minutes.
When a knife comes out clean, the cake is ready.

7. Remove from oven and allow to cool.

8. For the icing, mix together butter, icing sugar and cocoa. When the cake is cool,
use one third of your icing to stick both halves together.
Use the remaining icing to cover the top and sides.

9. Eat and enjoy!